The Teacher Who Would Not Retire
Goes to Camp

Story by Sheila & Letty Sustrin
Illustrations by Thomas H. Boné III

Blue Marlin Publications

The Teacher Who Would Not Retire
Goes To Camp

Published by Blue Marlin Publications

Text copyright © 2005 by Sheila & Letty Sustrin

Illustrations copyright © 2005 by Francine Poppo Rich

First printing 2005

Library of Congress Cataloging-in-Publication Data

Sustrin, Sheila.
 The teacher who would not retire goes to camp / story by Sheila & Letty Sustrin ;
illustrations by Thomas H. Boné III.
   p. cm.
 Summary: When a retired teacher substitutes as a summer camp teacher, she
learns not to wear ballet slippers for hiking or fishing.
 ISBN-13: 978-0-9674602-7-7 (hardcover : alk. paper)
 ISBN-10: 0-9674602-7-1 (hardcover : alk. paper)
 [1. Teachers--Fiction. 2. Camps--Fiction. 3. Ballet slippers--Fiction.] I. Sustrin, Letty.
 II. Boné, Thomas H., ill. III. Title.

 PZ7.S96584Tea 2005
 [E]--dc22
                              2005005237

Blue Marlin Publications, Ltd.
823 Aberdeen Road, West Bay Shore, NY 11706
www.bluemarlinpubs.com

Printed and bound by Aegean Offset Printers
Book design & layout by Jude Rich

For
Francine and Jude Rich
Our "Life After Retirement" career was made possible because
of your support, guidance, and friendship.
Thank you.
-LS & SS

To My Wife, daughter, mother, and father, whose wonderful support made
my contribution to this book possible.

- THB

On the last day of school,
as the bus left with the
children, Mrs. Belle waved
goodbye and called out, "Have
a wonderful summer vacation,
children."

Mr. Rivera, the Principal, shouted,
"Have a great time at the Laurelville
Sleep-Away Camp."

Then he turned to Mrs. Belle and said, "Wait until the children get to camp on Monday. They are going to be so surprised to see me there. I'm the new owner."

"I'm going to have a quiet summer," said Mrs. Belle. "I will spend time finding books to read to the children next year. I also have to buy some new ballet slippers for Reading Day."

On Monday morning, Mr. Rivera sat on the steps of the Camp House. With his head in his hand, he kept saying, "Oh my, what am I going to do? My Head Teacher broke her leg and won't be coming. I need someone to show the counselors what to do with the children every day. How can I disappoint them?"

Suddenly, Wendy, the camp cook, came running out of the building, calling, "Mr. Rivera! Mr. Rivera! Don't worry! The Head Teacher just called. She's sending her aunt, a retired teacher, to take her place. She's coming on the camp bus with the children."

"What wonderful news, and just in time. Here comes the bus now," said Mr. Rivera.

As they got off the bus, the children were wearing their camp outfits and sneakers. They were so excited to see Mr. Rivera.

"Welcome to the Laurelville Sleep-Away Camp. Do you like my surprise? I'm the new owner of the camp," said Mr. Rivera.

"We do like your surprise Mr. Rivera, but we have a surprise for you, too!"

"Here's our new Head Camp Teacher," said the children. They all pointed to the steps of the bus.

Mr. Rivera took one look and said, "I don't believe what I see! I think this is going to be a very interesting summer."

There on the step was a pair of feet wearing red ballet slippers—not the camp sneakers. It was Mrs. Belle!

Mr. Rivera announced:

MRS. BELLE, THIS WILL NOT DO! YOU MUST WEAR THE PROPER SHOE!

Mrs. Belle just gave him a great, big smile.

The boys followed Mr. Rivera to the cabin marked *Boys*, and the girls went with Mrs. Belle into the other cabin. There were bunk beds. The last bed, which was left for Mrs. Belle, was on top.

Mrs. Belle opened her backpack and took out a hammer and five hooks. She climbed the ladder and hung the hooks across the side of her bed.

"What are the hooks for?" asked one of the girls.

Mrs Belle smiled and pulled out five colorful pairs of ballet slippers from her backpack. She hung each pair on a hook.

Suddenly, there was a loud noise. Everyone ran outside, and there was Mr. Rivera, ringing a huge bell. He called out, "Put on your hiking shoes. We're going to have a picnic in the forest. I'm the leader. Everyone will follow me."

Mrs. Belle responded, "I'll be the last one in line so no one gets lost."

Mrs. Belle went back to her cabin to get ready. Then Mr. Rivera looked down at her feet and asked, "Mrs. Belle, where are your hiking shoes?"

Mr. Rivera shook his finger at her and said, "You'll be sorry."

They followed Mr. Rivera up the hill and down the other side. Poor Mrs. Belle. She had such a hard time keeping up. The ground was muddy, and her ballet slippers were getting wet.

The wagon got stuck on a rock. As Mrs. Belle yanked the wagon, she slipped and landed in the road. The wagon turned over, and all the food fell out.

Meanwhile, Mr. Rivera and the children arrived at the picnic area. Mr. Rivera said, "What wonderful hikers you all are. I know how hungry you must be. Let's eat now." He called out, "Mrs. Belle, you may give out the food."

There was no answer. Everyone turned and looked. Where was Mrs. Belle? She had disappeared.

They started back and suddenly saw Mrs. Belle in the middle of the road. Luckily, she was not hurt.

Mr. Rivera bent down to pull her up, but Mrs. Belle grabbed his hand so hard that he fell down in the mud, too. When he stood, the strawberry shortcake was on top of his head.

Mr. Rivera said:

MRS. BELLE, THIS WILL NOT DO!
YOU MUST WEAR A HIKING SHOE!

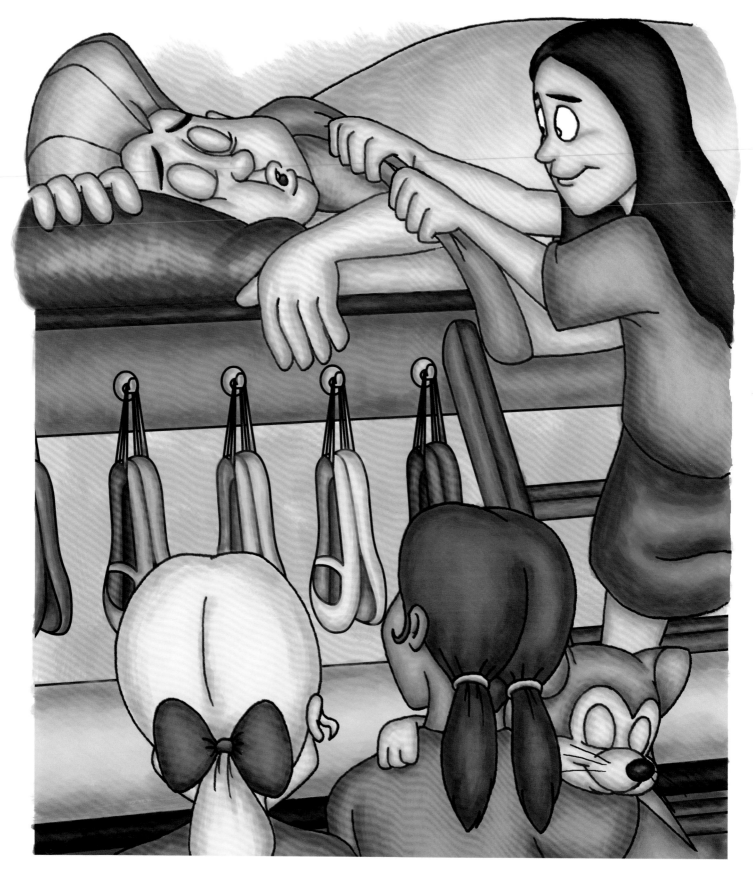

That night, Mrs. Belle was so tired that the girls had to push her up the ladder into her bed.

She fell fast asleep and was awakened suddenly by the loud sound of Mr. Rivera's bell. "Time to get up," called Mr. Rivera.

"What!" moaned Mrs. Belle. "It's only six o'clock in the morning."

Mr. Rivera bellowed, "It's the best time of day to go fishing and snorkeling. Put on your swimsuits, eat breakfast, and meet me at the dock at seven o'clock."

As they got to the dock, Mr. Rivera held some fishing poles. "All those who want to fish, come over here. If you want to snorkel, go to Mrs. Belle. Snorkelers MUST wear goggles and flippers."

The children hurried to get ready to go into the lake. Mr. Rivera looked down at Mrs. Belle's feet and said, "Where are your flippers?"

She answered, "My pink ballet slippers will be fine!"

Mr. Rivera folded his arms and said, "You'll be sorry."

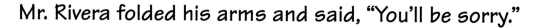

A little while later, one boy shouted, "I caught a fish. It must be a big fish. It must be a VERY BIG FISH! I need help."

Mr. Rivera and the children pulled and pulled, as the fish tugged and tugged on the line. "Oh my, this fish must weigh at least 100 pounds," said Mr. Rivera. "I didn't know we had such big fish in our lake."

"Here it comes," yelled the children.

Mr. Rivera took one look and said, "Oh no, I don't believe it."

Hanging upside down from the fishing pole was Mrs. Belle. Her pink ballet slipper, with her big toe sticking out, was caught on the hook.

Mr. Rivera said:

MRS. BELLE, THIS WILL NOT DO!
YOU MUST WEAR A SNORKELING SHOE!

Poor Mrs. Belle. That night, while everyone had fun sitting around the campfire, she sat with her sore toe soaking in a tub of water.

The next morning, it was raining. Mr. Rivera said, "Boys and girls, I have a special treat for you. We're all going bowling."

At the bowling alley, each child was given a pair of bowling shoes. Mrs. Belle was still wearing ballet slippers. Mr. Rivera asked, "Mrs. Belle, where are your bowling shoes?"

She answered, "My purple ballet slippers will be just fine!"

Mr. Rivera shook his finger again and said, "You'll be sorry."

The children formed teams, and they started to bowl. Mrs. Belle picked a green ball and slowly moved to the foul line. As she went to throw the ball, her ballet slippers started to slide down the alley.

"Look," shouted one of the boys. "Mrs. Belle is dancing down the bowling alley."

"Oh no! I can't look," said Mr. Rivera.

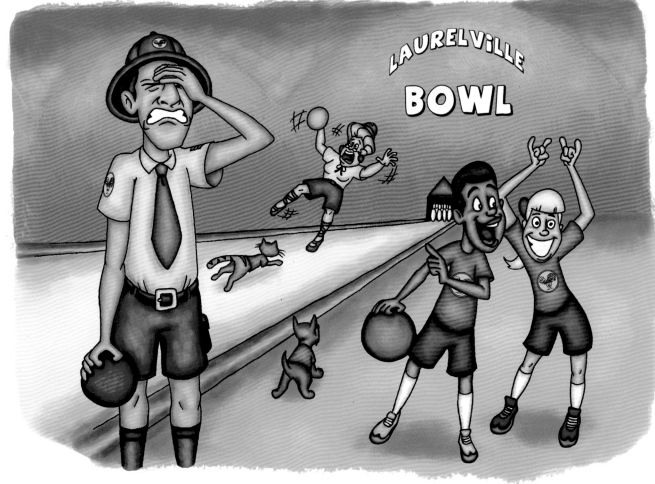

As Mrs. Belle reached the bowling pins, she slid into them and knocked all ten down. "Hooray!" shouted the children on her team. "Mrs. Belle made a strike. She won the game for us."

Now Mr. Rivera yelled:

MRS. BELLE, THIS WILL NOT DO!
YOU MUST WEAR A BOWLING SHOE!

When they arrived back at camp, Mr. Rivera looked very angry. The children heard him tell Mrs. Belle he wanted to meet with her in the morning. They were worried that he would send her home.

That night, while Mrs. Belle and Mr. Rivera were asleep, the boys and girls tiptoed quietly out of their cabins. They had a secret meeting with Wendy in the cafeteria to see how they could convince Mrs. Belle to wear safe shoes. After whispering for a long time, the children smiled. Wendy said, "You've come up with a perfect plan. I'll go into town tomorrow and get all the supplies you'll need."

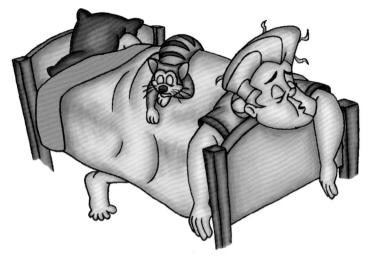

Poor Mrs. Belle. She was so sore the next morning that she had to stay in bed all day. Her meeting with Mr. Rivera had to be canceled.

While she slept, the Cook brought back a big box from town. The children took it and disappeared into the Art Room. They worked together all day, and finally they were done.

Then they put up a sign:

ALL INVITED!
IMPORTANT MEETING
AT
MRS. BELLE'S CABIN
7:00 PM

PLEASE COME!

After dinner, everyone marched into Mrs. Belle's cabin. The children said:

"Mrs. Belle, you must know, we want you happy, we love you so.
When you're hiking, you must wear shoes. If you slip, we'll hear sad news.
We love your ballet slippers, but when snorkeling, you must wear flippers.
When you throw that bowling ball, wear bowling shoes so you won't fall.
We've solved the problem for you, and Mr. Rivera is happy, too!"

Then they gave Mrs. Belle three big boxes. As she opened them, she began to cry. She was so happy that the children cared so much about her.

The boxes had new hiking shoes, flippers, and bowling shoes. But, not just plain ones. The children had decorated all three pairs with stickers and magic marker drawings of colorful ballet slippers. Now everyone would know by the designs on them that it was still Mrs. Belle.

Mr. Rivera announced:

MRS. BELLE, YES, THIS WILL DO!
NOW YOU'LL WEAR THE PROPER SHOE!

Then Mrs. Belle handed everyone a box, as she said:

"To all my friends, big and small,
Tomorrow night we'll have a ball.
We'll dance the whole night through,
And YOU will have the proper shoe!"

And they all danced.

MRS. BELLES
CAT

THE
NURSE DISGUISE

THE CONSTRUCTION
WORKER DISGUISE

THE
TRAPEZE
ARTIST
DISGUISE

NO
DISGUISE!
THE ORIGINAL
MRS. BELLE

THE
JAZZ
PLAYER
DISGUISE